OTHERWORLDLY

CAROLINE SCOTT

Otherworldly Copyright©

2021 by Caroline Scott

All rights reserved.

The characters in this book are entirely fictional. Any resemblance to actual places or persons living or dead is entirely coincidental.

✸ Created with Vellum

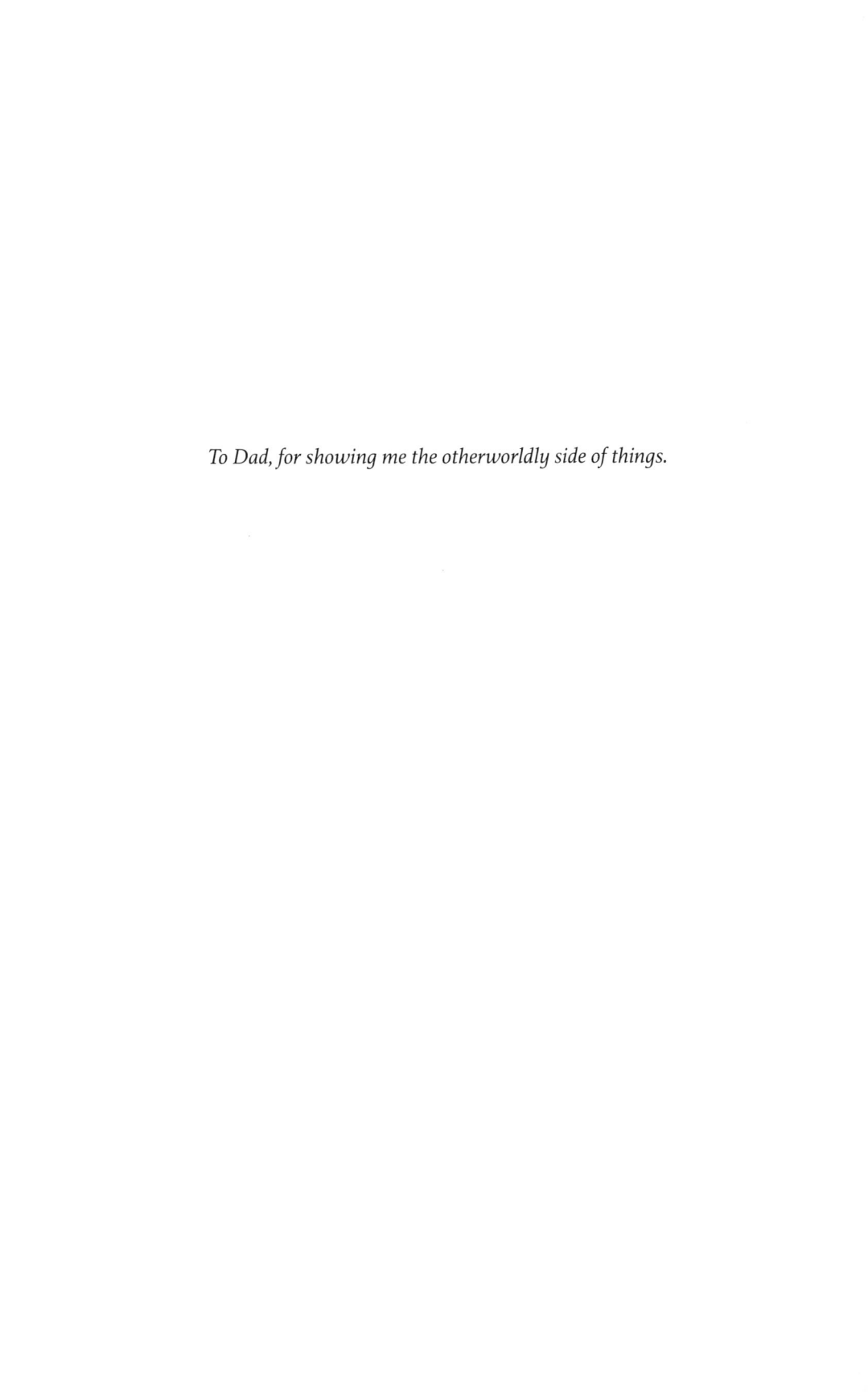

To Dad, for showing me the otherworldly side of things.

THEME SONG

Let Love In – Goo Goo Dolls

QUOTE

"Follow your bliss and the universe will open doors where there were only walls."
　　Joseph Campbell

1
OPAL

"Hey, Opal!" These words welcome me nearly every morning as I enter Beans N' Books. I roll my eyes and wait for Eli Whitlock to tell his daily joke. They're never very good.

"How did the hipster burn his tongue?" Eli asks me as he pours a bag of beans into one of the coffee machines.

"I don't know. How?" I say uninterested as I climb the steps to the second floor.

"He drank his coffee before it was cool!" He yells the answer since I'm halfway up the steps. I hear his muffled laughter when I reach the top. I inhale the smell of wood and old books and smile.

My best friend, Abbie, manages the shop, and her aunt owns it. Six months ago, before the store opened, Abbie's aunt, Clara, asked me if I wanted to open my own library on the second floor, hence the name Beans N' Books. I eagerly obliged because I've always wanted to own a bookstore, library, or something of the sort. And I get to work with my best friend.

Abbie and I have been friends ever since we could walk. In high school, we always dreamed of working together and being roommates. We've accomplished one of those. As for being roommates, that's a work in progress. I've been hesitant to leave my parents' house because we're so close. Abbie currently lives with her aunt and is waiting for me to make the move.

I set my purse down on my desk and power on my computer. I open a file that contains a list of books due back in the library today, and then I check my email to see if anyone is scheduled to donate any books this week. My inbox is empty, so I begin to shelve books.

"Pick a card?" I jolt and drop the books I have in my hand. I get so lost in the quiet up here that I startle easily. One hardcover book hits my foot. *Ouch.*

"Shit. Sorry." Eli helps me pick up the fallen books. Well, this is a new one. He's got magic tricks *and* jokes?

"Thanks," I mumble.

"No problem." He fans out the deck of tarot cards for me to pick from.

Oh. Tarot cards? Why does he have tarot cards?

No one can deny the beauty that is Eli Whitlock. As I reach for a card, his brown eyes latch onto mine and the corner of his mouth turns up, displaying his single dimple on his left cheek. It's hard for me to say no to him, no matter how terrible his joke telling is.

I pull out a card from the deck and hand it to him. As he examines the face of the card, I cross my arms like the skeptic I am.

"Ah...the High Priestess." He closes his eyes in concentration. I almost laugh; I've never believed in anything related to clairvoyance or the supernatural.

He tilts his head to the side as if he's trying to remember something. "You have some feelings that you're not letting out. It's like you're pushing them down to get rid of them."

His eyes remain closed. I look up at him and then at the card. He's not wrong.

My mom is refusing to quit her job, even though her boss is treating her horribly for no reason whatsoever. I've mentioned it to her time and time again, but she doesn't want to hear any of it. See, I'm trying not to meddle, but it's hard. I don't like anyone treating my mom with less respect than she deserves.

So, I nod. "Interesting..." I resume putting the books away.

Eli starts to say something, but then, "ELI!" That's Abbie. She must need him for something downstairs.

Eli shuffles the cards and quickly puts them back into their box. "See ya, Opal."

I give him a small wave and watch as he jogs down the creaky steps.

Someone once told me that it's not the actual card reader or psychic who predicts your future or knows your feelings. Apparently, it's your own energy being reflected, and that's how the results are produced; I don't know if I believe that either though.

I hear hard, determined footsteps as someone comes up the stairs. Abbie. She shakes her head. "Eli... Always distracted." She sighs, pulls up a wooden barstool, and sits beside me at the desk.

I laugh. "Yeah, and now he's trying to give people card readings."

"Oh, I *know*. But I actually dig that," Abbie says. I quirk a brow, and she continues, "I've always loved wooey-wooey shit. You know that. So, of course I picked a card."

"Well?" I straighten a few loose papers on my desk. I refrain from telling her that I, too, picked a card.

Excited, Abbie sits up straighter. "He said the card I picked meant that I was having vivid nightmares about Teletubbies as of late. It's true. I mean, who would just pull that out of their ass?"

I laugh. "Okay, Abbie."

She slaps a hand on my desk. "One day, you'll believe. I know it."

I roll my eyes playfully and go back to looking up something on my computer. She sticks her tongue out at me and skips down the stairs.

It would take a miracle for me to believe in anything "wooey-wooey."

2
OPAL

Some would call me a pessimist, and maybe they'd be right. My dad is an architect, and my mom is a painter, but do *I* have an ounce of creativity running through my bloodstream? No. I love to read, and I love the idea of writing, but whenever I sit down and try to write, I end up writing the same story about a crazy cat lady. It stops there; my mind draws a blank. So I recently joined a writing club to try to spark some creativity. This will be my first time attending. I'll be sitting there all awkward, surrounded by creatives. I don't mind being around groups of people; it's the *speaking* that I'm not excited about. But my wanting to write trumps that fear, so I made the decision to try it out. I try not to think about it as I drive to the town library, where the group meets.

When I arrive, there is quite a large number of cars in the parking lot. I enter the building through the sliding doors at the front. A corkboard near the entrance displays all the library's events. I peer at the board to see which room the group is meeting in. "Meeting Room 1," it reads. I look around and find a hallway that has "Meeting Room 1" in bold letters on the wall.

As I near the room, I hear mumbled discussion. My heart

starts racing, and I scold myself for it. I round the corner into the room and stop dead in my tracks.

Eli.

I had no idea he was involved with this group. I just Googled "writing group + Eldridge, Washington," and it led me here.

Eli is sitting in a chair in the center of the small room. About seven other attendants sitting in their own chairs form a circle around him. He's in the middle of telling a story, when he sees me and waves his arms dramatically.

"Hey, Opal!" he exclaims, surprise on his face. I give him a small wave and watch as he gets up, strolls over to a stack of chairs in the corner of the room, and grabs one.

As he situates the chair for me, he says, "What do you call a place that's full of writers?"

Oh, dear God. "What?" I cross my arms and quirk a brow.

"A writer's block." His words roll into a laugh.

A few people in the circle look from him to me, confused.

I point a finger at him. "Good one," I say sarcastically. He must have a joke for everything.

He ignores me and clasps his hands. "Everyone, this is Opal."

His introduction is met with smiles and waves. I smile back at the circle of writers. I am torn between backing out and staying. I don't hate Eli or anything; it just feels weird seeing him here. I never knew he liked to write. What if I suck at writing? I'm not gonna lie: I now feel extra pressure to *impress him.* Before coming, I just felt nervous about speaking in front of a group; this has progressed to a whole other level.

I remember that this was the only writers' group I could find in Eldridge, so I pull myself together and take my seat beside a woman who's holding two overstuffed notebooks.

I hope we don't have to read out loud.

I brought a notebook with me, but there is no way in *hell* that

I'm going to read my unfinished crazy cat lady story to all of these people—especially him.

Eli walks over to the small whiteboard in the center of the room and uncaps a red marker. *Great. He's the leader of the group.*

"For our newcomers..." He winks at me, and I flush. He continues, "Every meeting, I put a topic on the board for you to write about—just one word—and then you can write whatever you'd like about that word. This is an exercise to boost inspiration and help improve your writing. I'm always here if you have any questions or if you'd like my opinion on what you wrote. Remember, this class is for fun."

I relax a little at the word "fun." He turns his back to us and begins writing a word on the board. I dig through my purse and grab my notebook. I look back up at the board and stifle a laugh. The word he wrote is "toothbrush." How does he expect us to write about a toothbrush?

He caps the marker. "Remember, guys, it can be about anything. It can be about using a toothbrush, buying a toothbrush...a *talking* toothbrush. Let your imagination take over."

I grip the pen and stare at the blank page in my lap. A few more minutes of this go by, and then Eli comes over, bends down beside my chair, and whispers, "I didn't expect to see you here."

"I could say the same about you," I whisper back while the other writers scribble away. Pens and pencils scratching against paper is the only sound.

He reaches into his back pocket and pulls out his old tarot cards.

This again?

"Pick a card," he whispers, fanning out the deck.

"Can't you see I'm trying to write about toothbrushes?" I whisper-hiss. He eyes the blank page and I grip my pen. I release my grip as I follow his gaze.

"I can see that you've got nothing written down. Maybe a card will give you some inspiration."

I roll my eyes and pick a card.

"It's the star...reversed," he informs me. I give him a questioning look. "When the star card is reversed, it means you may be feeling discouraged or insecure about something." He looks around the room—everyone is still scribbling away—and then back at me. "I'd say that's accurate."

I hate it, 'cause it's true. I shoot him a glare. *Asshole.*

He smiles slyly and proceeds to walk around the room.

At the end of the session, when everyone is packing up their things, I stare at the open page in my notebook. I ended up writing the world "toothbrush" over and over again in hopes that I would think of something. I sigh and begin packing up my things. As I'm about to shoulder my purse and leave, I notice Eli waiting at the door, looking straight at me. I make my way to the door, ready to get out of there.

"Opal." Eli's voice is gentle. I meet his eyes. "I'm glad you came. You will write something great. I'll make sure of it."

I offer him a small smile and nod before I exit into the pouring rain.

This should be interesting.

3

OPAL

Abbie hugs the tub of popcorn as she leans over in the passenger seat, erupting with laughter. I stare wide-eyed at the popcorn as it begins to make its descent all over my car. Well, my *mom's* car.

"Abbie!" My reprimand is partnered with a giggle. She hugs the popcorn more tightly and shrugs.

"Sorry, Op. It was funny." She stuffs a handful of popcorn into her mouth.

"Give me that!" My smile widens as I snatch the bag of popcorn from her. I end up being the one to get greasy popcorn all over the car. Our simultaneous gasps are followed by our high-pitched laughter.

"Shh!" Someone hisses from a car parked a few spots down from us. Abbie and I look at each other, our faces red from the strain of holding back our laughter.

She and I frequent the drive-in every Friday night regardless of what movie is playing. Tonight, it's an old film involving psychics and ghosts. Abbie, of course, is loving every minute of it. She actually believes in that stuff. I'm enjoying it because one of my favorite pastimes is laughing at cheesy old movies with my best friend.

"Asshole," I whisper to myself and look back at the person who dared to shush us.

Abbie nudges me in my side. "We were the ones being the assholes. You can't hit pause at a drive-in." Abbie is a people pleaser, unlike me, but she does have a point.

I shrug and grab a handful of popcorn out of the bag.

Abbie shakes her head, her black curls swaying with the movement. "I can't believe you don't believe in psychics *or* ghosts."

She reaches into the bag as I say, "I won't believe it until I see it."

I hear her mumble under her breath "Have a little faith, Op."

As we turn our attention back to the movie, I notice a short, stocky younger guy approach us. Abbie slouches dramatically in her seat. The top of my mom's car, a candy-red convertible, is wide open as we watch the movie. I make eye contact with the guy as he strolls over to Abbie's side of the car. Abbie slouches down even more until her head is barely visible. She looks at me and then back at the guy, an exasperated expression on her face. The guy approaches the vehicle and bends down so he's eye level with Abbie, who just stares straight ahead, not engaging.

Before the guy can even open his mouth, I blurt, "She's a lesbian."

He meets my eyes, and his cheeks turn pink as he quickly walks back toward his group of friends. They pat him on the back and bring their fists up to their mouths, laughing at his embarrassment.

"Thank you." Abbie sighs, straightening up in her seat. I squeeze her hand in response. "Leah would've killed him." She laughs softly.

Leah is Abbie's girlfriend, and they've been together for

nearly three years now. Leah is a force of nature. Her presence shines brightly wherever she goes, and no one dares to screw with her or her girlfriend. I smile softly at the memory of her beating up a creepy guy for even looking at Abbie. It makes me feel good knowing Abbie is protected and loved.

When the movie ends, we drive back to Abbie's house. She turns up the radio when a Matchbox Twenty song comes on. My thick red hair blows around me, and I breathe in the cool night air. A sense of peace comes over me. I glance over at Abbie and smile, watching her belt out lyrics in the dead of night.

When we arrive at the house, Abbie's aunt, Clara, greets us as we make our way inside the small, one-story brick house. Clara notices our wind-swept air and laughs lightly. We climb the stairs to Abbie's bedroom. Every time I enter this room, thousands of memories flow through my mind. Whispers of childhood crushes, homework, prom, breakup aftermaths... You name it, it's gone down in this bedroom.

I plop on the bright pink bedspread as Abbie rummages through her drawers for her tub full of nail polishes. This girl has every color nail polish you can think of. She holds up bright red polish in one hand and black in the other, silently asking me which color I want. I point at the black one. My nails shall be black like my soul. Abbie tosses me a sunny yellow color for her.

She then grabs two old newspapers from another tub and places them flat on the bed. She shakes the black nail polish in one hand as she situates herself across from me. I place my hand flat on the newspaper. She unscrews the cap of the nail polish remover, braces a cotton ball against the opening, and turns the bottle upside down. She begins to remove my old polish.

"So?" Abbie asks, waiting for me to spill the latest news on Opal O'Connell.

I sigh. "So, you know I was going to attend a writing group, right?"

Abbie nods, her eyes narrowed in concentration as she scrubs polish off my thumb.

"Um…Eli leads the group." Abbie pauses and looks up at me as if looking for something on my face. She doesn't seem surprised since Eldridge is such a small town. I force myself to push down the heat that creeps its way up my cheeks.

"And how do we feel about that?" She uncaps the new polish.

I shrug. "It's annoying. It's like he knows what I'm thinking all the time."

"Right. 'Cause he's psychic. Duh." Abbie giggles. I wouldn't be surprised if she legitimately believed that.

I shake my head in an attempt to drop the conversation. I'm still processing the situation myself. But despite myself, I say, "I feel all vulnerable around him. I don't like it."

Abbie shoots me a knowing grin.

"What?" I'm slightly irritated.

"Oh, nothing. Just keep me updated on the situation, Op."

She screws the cap back on the polish, and I nod before I blow on my freshly painted nails.

4
ELI

"Ouch!" Felix growls in irritation as the third chopstick floats through the room and hits the back of his head with a thwack.

"Bro!" Dawson, who's huddled next to Felix on the small love seat in the apartment I share with August, picks up one of the chopsticks off the ground and chucks it back at August, who catches it effortlessly and laughs.

"Enough," I say sternly as I pick through the beef and broccoli on my plate. My cousins and I get together every week for Chinese food, our favorite cuisine. I'm the eldest at twenty-three; August is twenty-one; and Felix and Dawson, fraternal twins, are seventeen. We all have some sort of psychic ability, passed down through the Whitlock male family line for ages, and mine constantly gives me a throbbing mental headache, literally and figuratively. Our specific gifts have been passed down through our fathers or grandfathers. Whenever our uncles are not present with us, I'm in charge.

As for our psychic abilities, I was gifted with clairsentience, which is an intuitive ability that allows me to feel what others are feeling without them telling me. So, I'm great at tarot readings. I correlate the card's meaning with what someone is feeling.

August was gifted with telekinesis, which means he can move objects, such as chopsticks, across a room without touching them. Mind control. August and I can also communicate telepathically, which we've practiced since we were little. Our dads and uncles thought since we're the oldest of the Whitlock boys, it might do some good down the line, which it has.

Felix is a psychic medium, which gives him the ability to communicate with the dead. His dad, Clark, doesn't want him doing any readings until he is eighteen. When he does begin to offer readings, he will act as a medium between his clients and those who have passed on. He's still honing his gift.

Dawson has the psychic ability of precognition, which allows him to see events that haven't happened yet. Right now, his visions are blurry, but like Felix, he is still honing his gift. Dawson inherited his gift from their dad, while Felix inherited his from their grandfather.

Felix and Dawson are more inclined to get involved in romantic relationships since they're the youngest out of all of us and don't have as much responsibility. August and I, being the oldest, have little to no luck in that department because we have to be there for each other and the twins if something goes wrong or if we need to talk to someone about our abilities. August, Felix, and Dawson feel more comfortable coming to me than going to their fathers for advice and so on. This is fine, but it does take its toll. Our fathers—Charles, Henry, and Clark—own a psychic business that's always bustling with clients. They even travel for readings and conferences with other psychics. I love these boys, and I'd go to the ends of the earth for each one of them. But damn, are they a lot of work.

I think about my writing group, which I formed two years ago. I wanted to branch out and help people in a different, more human way instead of being holed up in the psychic world that my family lives in. I love doing tarot readings for clients, but I was craving something more.

I love running the writing group. I've made connections with the people who attend; some of them have been with me for the whole two years. I keep my abilities separate from my classes. Even if my students don't know it, I don't want to barge in on their feelings when they're just trying to be creative. It feels wrong, and there's no point. It's healthier for me not to use my abilities during sessions.

But that all changed when Opal showed up. I shift in my chair, uncomfortable with the thought, when August flicks my ear. I blink out of my trance.

"Hello?" August says to me. "I was asking you a question, and after my third attempt at trying to get your attention, I had to resort to the flick."

Oh, August. He causes the most trouble out of all of us. "What's your question?" I turn my body so I'm facing him.

"Are you in love?" His question shocks me.

I flash him an incredulous look that says *As if.* "No." I glance at Dawson and Felix.

"Then give me a good reason you're so distracted." August twirls a chopstick between his long, slender fingers.

I snatch the chopstick from his grasp and place it gently on the table. I automatically get in a mood whenever someone interrupts my thoughts. I begin to close my mind to make sure he can't try to communicate with me telepathically. "There's a new drink at work that I have to learn to make. It's hard."

"Right." August purses his lips, sensing the lie. He gets up from the table and heads over to the twins.

My thoughts drift back to long red hair and green eyes.

5

OPAL

I don't know if it's because I've had time to process the whole thing, but I actually feel nervous as I drive the short distance to the library for the weekly session. I don't even know if "nervous" is the correct word for this feeling. It's not as if Eli himself makes me nervous; plus, feeling nervous is not a feeling I'm met with often.

I pull up to the library, gather my things from the passenger seat, and head inside. As soon as I enter the small room, I notice that Eli is talking with one of the writers. I take my seat and begin to pull out my notebook and pen.

"Hey, Opal." I glance up from my notebook to see him looking at me. Relief appears on his face. "Did you hear about the writer who became a baker?"

I have no idea how he comes up with these jokes. "No."

"Well, they say he makes excellent synonym rolls." He winks at me and continues talking with the other writer. My insides flutter; I'm not sure whether it's from the bad joke or the wink.

Eli approaches the front of the room and uncaps his dry-erase marker. He scribbles a word on the board and uses his free hand to shield it so that we can't see what he is writing.

"Our word for today is 'red.' This is a broad writing prompt, so let your imagination run wild." He pushes the cap closed on the marker and sets it on the white board's metal tray.

I tap my pen lightly on my notebook, which rests on my lap. The thing about these one-word prompts is that I overthink what I can write about since it's only one word. If the prompt were a sentence or two, that would probably be a different story. I sigh in frustration. I push the pen firmly into the paper and write the word "red" in bold letters.

The scent of spearmint and patchouli consume me as Eli crouches down next to me. I feel my body tense at his unexpected closeness.

He seems to sense my struggle. "What is your favorite thing that is the color red?"

I think about this for a moment, trying not to let his presence distract me. Spaghetti," I say. Of course, my mind goes straight to food. My stomach tightens as it threatens to let out an embarrassing growl, which I know the whole room will hear.

"Good," Eli says. "Write about that."

How am I supposed to write about spaghetti? I look around to see everyone else writing away as usual.

Eli sighs and runs a hand through his thick, shoulder-length brown hair. I eye him curiously. "Why don't we get some spaghetti after class?" His eyes meet mine and then divert to the carpet beneath our feet.

"I-I..." I'm at a loss for words. His brown eyes meet mine once more.

"As friends, of course." A warm grin spreads over his face, his dimple making an appearance.

"Uh...yeah. Sure." I offer him a small smile. I tell myself that I accepted the offer because of the hunger taking over me, but in reality, I can't say no to those brown eyes. I curse myself for sounding so pathetic.

"Great." He stands up.

"Great." I purse my lips. My cheeks burn.

I end up writing a paragraph about the time I attempted to make spaghetti for my parents and burned it. It's only a paragraph, but at least it's not the cat lady story, so I try to be happy with it. I'm honestly surprised that I was able to form words on paper or otherwise after Eli's invite. On sentence two, my mind started its overthinking loop, revolving around dimples and bad jokes.

The session ends, and as I'm packing up my things, Eli approaches me.

"Lorenzo's or Valentina's?" He names the only two decent Italian restaurants in town.

"Lorenzo's," I reply without hesitation.

"Good taste." He flips his car keys around his fingers with effortless grace.

As we make our way out, he opens the library door for me, and we start walking toward his car.

"Write anything cool about spaghetti?" he asks me.

I let out a small laugh and look up at him. "A paragraph about how I burned it."

His eyes latch onto mine, sincerity coating his features. "That's great, Opal. Every writer starts somewhere, and you did it all on your own." He bumps his shoulder against mine, and a charming smile plays on his lips.

"I wouldn't have written anything if I hadn't shown up to your group," I tell him honestly.

He shrugs. "I find that hard to believe. You've got creativity brewing inside you, anxiously waiting to come out."

I blush, not really knowing how to respond. I settle on "Thanks."

When we reach his Subaru, he opens the passenger door for

me. An unfamiliar feeling washes over me, and I stop for a moment. A guy has never opened a car door for me.

"Opal?" Eli notices my pause.

I look up at him and grin. "Thank you" is all I say as I climb into the seat.

Eli's car smells of spearmint and something woodsy, it's a comforting smell. I relax against the passenger seat, despite my nerves about going out to eat with my *very* attractive co-worker. During the drive, we talk and laugh about rude customers at work. An easy topic, thankfully.

We park in front of the quaint restaurant, and Eli makes a point to get out before me and, once again, open my door. I awkwardly step out of the car. I can't see myself getting used to this.

We step inside the cozy restaurant, and the aroma of spices and pizza dough fills my nostrils. I smile at the familiar scents. My stomach finally emits that unruly growl that was itching to be let out at the library. Eli raises his thick brows at me in response, and I laugh.

The hostess leads us to a small table in the back corner of the restaurant.

"Thanks for inviting me. I'm starving." I eye the huge menu, already knowing exactly what I want, as I've been to this restaurant many times before.

"Sure. Spaghetti sounded delicious when you said it, and I haven't been here in ages." He looks around the dimly lit restaurant, slaps the menu down next to him, and leans forward. "You already know what you want. Why are you still looking at the menu?" A taunting grin plays on his lips.

Embarrassed, I glower at him over the top of the menu. *How did he know that? Am I that transparent?* I can hear Abbie's voice in my head, *'Cause he's psychic. Duh.*

I laugh softly to myself and set the menu aside.

The waitress comes back to take our orders: spaghetti with marinara sauce and extra garlic sticks for me and spaghetti with meatballs for Eli. We thank her as she collects our menus. When she turns away, Eli stares at me, his eyes slightly narrowed.

"Uh, can I help you?" I take a sip of water.

"Yes. Pick a card." He fishes his box of tarot cards from his pocket. He really does take them everywhere.

I oblige as he fans out the colorful cards. I pull one from the end and place it facedown on the table. He slides the card closer to him and flips it over.

"The death card." His eyes twinkle. My eyes widen at the word "death." I shake my head. I don't believe in that stuff anyways.

"New beginnings. It's not what you think. Many people think that the death card is bad, given the name, but nope. If the card is reversed, maybe. But since it's not, this could mean new beginnings with your writing…or something else." I note his hesitation before the words "something else." I nod slowly.

"You really don't believe in this stuff, do you?" He fiddles with his straw wrapper.

"No, I don't. If something is bigger than me or hard for me to understand, it's hard for me to believe in it," I tell him truthfully.

"Hm." He takes a gulp of his water. "What if I explained it or showed you more?"

I eye him, curious. "More what?"

He's about to answer me when the front door to Lorenzo's opens. Eli, who is facing the door, glares at whoever just entered. I cinch my eyebrows in confusion and turn around in my seat to see who his glare is being directed at. There's a boy with short, wavy blond hair, and rings adorn his pale, slender fingers. He looks about nineteen or twenty. I turn back around to face Eli and raise my brow in question. They must know each other.

"Give me a minute, Opal." As he scoots his chair away from

the table, he continues to stare at the boy. He stands up and walks over to him.

The waitress brings our food, and I thank her before putting a big forkful of spaghetti in my mouth. With my mouth full, I turn around in my seat to watch the interaction between Eli and the boy.

"And you couldn't take care of it, August?" Eli's voice is low, and he sounds slightly angry. The boy's eyes flit to mine, and he winks. I divert my eyes and act as if I'm stretching my back. I casually watch them exchange hurried whispers for a couple more minutes before I turn back around.

Eli comes back to the table, and at the same time, the front door to Lorenzo's opens and shuts with force. I stick another forkful of spaghetti in my mouth and watch as Eli fidgets in his seat, eyes glued to the door.

Whatever this is seems important. "Eli? If you need to go, go. I'm good." I swallow the spaghetti.

He drags his eyes from the door to look at me. "Opal, look. I'm sorry. I've got younger cousins, and they're a handful. Uh, we'll do this again another time." He fishes a twenty and a ten out of his wallet and places the bills on the table. "I've got the meal. Thank you for coming with me. See ya at work."

I don't have time to reply as he grins apologetically and rushes out of the restaurant.

My mind swims through questions as I ask the waitress for two to-go boxes.

6
ELI

Ten years ago

"Why am I here again?" I look around at my dad and uncles. My dad, Charles, is leaning forward with his hands clasped, while my uncles, Henry and Clark, are slouched back in their chairs. Yesterday, they sat me down and told me that I had an ability—a *psychic* ability. My cousins and I have known about the Whitlock family psychics since we were born pretty much, and I've always known that there'd be a chance that I'd be "gifted," as they like to say. So, naturally, when I started recently involuntarily tapping into other people's emotions from across the room, I told them about it. Now, here we are.

My dad speaks first. "Think of this as practice to hone your ability."

Then Henry: "We're here for support." He lazily chews on a toothpick. He's been trying to curb his smoking habit.

Then Clark: "Our client is here for our services, *not* yours. Consider it like this: when you start a new job, you shadow someone, right? That's what this is."

I squeeze my palms together and look down at the floor.

"Well…what if I end up not wanting to conduct readings myself?"

I look up hesitantly and find my father and uncles exchanging looks.

Shit.

My dad claps his hands. He's wearing a warm smile. "Well, don't worry about that now." He checks his watch. "They should be here any moment."

They? I know I'm just observing, but I'm still nervous. What if I freak out? What if I'm overwhelmed by the feeling of their emotions?

Clark empties out the old water from the essential oil diffuser, refills it, and then applies a new oil. They always make sure the diffuser is running during readings; it's to "purify" the room—or something.

Henry stands, walks over to me, and pats my shoulder. Since his ability is telekinesis, he's not needed for this reading. I watch him discard his toothpick in the kitchen. *When is he ever needed for a reading?*

Ten minutes later, a soft knock sounds at the front door.

My dad winks at me and rises from his spot on the couch. I turn around in my chair and watch him open the door for the clients.

I stifle a laugh as I watch the couple step into the living room. I internally kick myself for wanting to laugh. The woman is very tall and has curly purple hair that is sticking up every which way as if it was done purposefully. The multiple bangles adorning each of her wrists jingle with each step she takes. The man is short, slim, and alarmingly normal looking next to the woman. I straighten and pull myself together.

"Thank you for coming. Please take a seat." My dad greets them warmly and guides them to the couch. The woman clutches the man's arm as they make their way over to it.

My dad and Clark take their seats across from the couple. Mercifully, the couple doesn't even look my way. My dad takes his time explaining his and Clark's abilities and how they will separately affect the reading.

The woman nods eagerly while the man's (I assume he is her husband) gaze wanders around the small living space. Clark shuffles the deck of tarot cards and carefully spreads them out on the table in front of them.

"Now... It's Ophelia, right?" My dad turns to the woman.

When she nods, he continues. "Ophelia, think of your intention for this reading today. Hover your hand over the cards slowly, and when you feel a pull to a certain card, take it out of the deck. You should feel a slight vibration or maybe even a chill when you reach the card."

Ophelia inhales deeply and slowly hovers her left hand over the cards. As I watch her hand pause on top of a card, I feel my throat closing. Caught off guard, I instinctively touch my throat, and then tears begin to prick my eyes. My dad makes quick eye contact with me before nodding toward the kitchen, where Henry is standing. I stand up from the couch, sadness and despair swallowing me whole. I cover my mouth to mask the choking sound threatening to rise, and I make my way over to my uncle. He pulls me close to him and guides me into the den. Three wooden desks are spread out in the small space. He motions for me to sit on the ottoman in the middle of the room, and he kneels down in front of me. Then, I let it all out. A strangled noise comes out of me, as it has been meaning to come out for years even though it's been five minutes. I keep telling myself it's Ophelia's emotions, not mine, but this doesn't stop the tears from falling. I lean on Henry's shoulder and fist his T-shirt tightly. He rubs my back.

In between my gasps, he whispers, "I'm going to teach you a trick. This will keep the emotions manageable, and if you'd like, it will keep them out entirely." My dad explained to me that these outbursts could happen during readings since my ability is still so new to me, but knowing the *why* doesn't make this feeling any less overwhelming.

I nod as he wipes the tears from my eyes with his thumb.

7
ELI

Present day

"I can't control it!" Felix tells me, panicking. He holds his face in his hands, and tears drip onto the coffee table. August interrupted my lunch with Opal because one of Felix's teachers called from school. Apparently, Felix seemed to be distracting the other kids. August and I know exactly why that is. His ability. August tells me that he's not comfortable around emotional stuff like this and isn't sure how to help. But in truth, he just doesn't want to deal with it, which is why he called me.

"Felix, look at me," I say gently. I squeeze his shoulder reassuringly. Felix slowly looks up, and his face is red and wet from crying. August stands behind us and awkwardly hands Felix a tissue.

"We're going to get through this together, okay?"

Felix nods and wipes his nose with the tissue.

I remember when I first found out I had psychic abilities. Getting used to feeling other people's emotions was exhausting as shit. So, I can understand to some degree what Felix is feeling; we all can. But only his father, Clark, will really know how to help him.

I stand up from my spot on the couch and pull my phone out of my pocket. I motion to August that I'm going to make a call, and he gives me a knowing look. I open the front door to our apartment and quietly shut it behind me. The soft wind rustles through my hair as I search my contacts. When I find Clark's name, I hit the "call" button. He answers on the first ring.

"Eli?" Clark's gruff voice causes me to turn the phone volume down.

"Hey, Uncle Clark. It's Felix."

There's a pause. "Is he okay? Is it about his ability?" Worry caresses the edges of Clark's voice. I hear boxes moving and people talking in the background; they must be at one of their events.

"Yes. I'm trying to comfort him. The school called this afternoon and said that Felix was causing a disturbance." My voice remains calm.

Clark curses softly. "We'll be back in town tomorrow. I'll talk with him then. I think it's time you show him how to close his mind. *You* show him; don't let August do it."

I pause. My dad and uncles haven't trusted me to teach any of my cousins to close their minds. It's a learning curve, and my uncles are experts at it. They've taught only August and me to do it. They prefer us to learn to control our abilities ourselves without the use of any "mind helpers," as they call it. Clark would do anything for his sons, as would my father and Uncle Henry, and Clark doesn't want Felix in any more pain than he's in right now. So, I guess desperate times call for desperate measures.

Clark and I go over the details of how to teach Felix, because it's been a long time since I've had to close my mind like how I'm about to show him.

"Thank you, Eli. We love you boys. We'll see you tomorrow.

Keep me updated on Felix, please." Clark hangs up before I can say goodbye.

I pocket my phone and head back into the apartment. August is still standing behind the couch, arms crossed over his chest as he just stares at Felix. Felix cracks his knuckles and stares at the floor. I walk back over to Felix and sit down next to him. I close my eyes briefly, remembering what Uncle Henry taught me.

"Felix? I need you to face me. I'm going to teach you something that's gonna help you, okay?" August shoots me a questioning glare. I ignore it. I'm glad Dawson is still at school, as he'd be upset about Felix learning something new without him. Felix shifts his body so that he's facing me.

"Tell me what you feel when you're at school," I say.

Felix clenches his jaw. "Whenever I'm talking or sitting next to friends, voices invade my head, and it's the voices of their family members who've passed on. It's only with my friends—no one else. Thank the Universe for that! But I can't have a normal conversation without hearing the voices, and they're *loud*, Eli. So, I avoid conversations or just zone out on them altogether. My friends are going to start thinking I'm crazy."

"No one's going to think you're crazy, Felix. Let me help you."

"What if it doesn't work?" Felix asks. August scoffs, and I glare at him.

"Leave the room. Now," I tell August. His presence could easily disrupt Felix while he's learning this new skill. August holds his hands up in surrender and strides to his bedroom at the end of the hall.

I turn my attention back to Felix. "It will, trust me. I use it sometimes." I give him a reassuring smile and ask him to close his eyes. He does.

"Now, imagine an open wooden double door with a white 'W' painted on each of the doors." The "W" has to be pictured for this to work. "W" is for Whitlock. Felix nods and shuts his eyes tighter. "Don't overthink it, buddy," I tell him. "Can you see the doors clearly?"

Felix nods again.

"Felix, I'm going to need you to communicate with someone, okay?"

For this to work, I need Felix to come in contact with someone I've personally lost. It can't be someone related to him as well, or this may not work. The goal is to get Felix to close his mind to unwanted visitors or voices, which are normally people he has no connection to—aka his friends' loved ones who have passed.

I think of the only person I've lost who Felix has no connection to—my ex-girlfriend, Lexi. Tears threaten to build in my eyes, but I tell myself that I need to be strong for Felix.

Lexi was my first serious girlfriend. We started dating when I was fifteen. A little more than a year into our relationship, she was killed in a plane crash while she and her volleyball team were on their way to an out-of-state tournament. Only two people survived the crash. I loved her. I was seventeen when she died, and Felix was eleven, so he didn't really know her.

When I found out about my ability, Lexi was the only person I confided in outside of my family, and she still loved and accepted me. She never judged me. She never judged anyone. She was my best friend, and I lost her in an instant. A silent tear rolls down my cheek, and I let it.

After she passed, I didn't talk to anyone for weeks. During my grieving period, my father taught me how to close my mind. I literally couldn't deal with my ability. I wasn't talking, sleeping, nor eating, and my father just couldn't let me go through Lexi's death on top of my newly discovered ability. When I was ready to open my mind back up, it was extremely difficult since it had been closed for so long, so I've had a lot of practice with it.

"Okay, Felix. I need you to focus on me now. Channel someone I've lost, just like you practiced with your dad when you first discovered your ability." My voice wavers slightly, but I recover.

Felix nods, and his whole face relaxes and remains like this for a few minutes. "She says she loves you and that she's proud of the man you've become. Do you know who this is? She's young. Her smile is bright." A small smile plays on his lips.

Another tear slips down my face. The selfish part of me wants to hear more, but the responsible cousin part of me continues with the lesson.

"Yes," I whisper. "Good, Felix. Now, picture the double door again." He nods, and his face tenses up a bit.

"Got it?" I ask, and when he nods again, I instruct, "Now, imagine the door closing, and do this slowly."

His angular face turns red with concentration.

"Relax, Felix, or this won't work."

He relaxes slightly at my words.

Moments later, a smile comes over his face. "I did it."

I smile too. "Good. Now slowly open your eyes." He does, and his eyes are as bright as Lexi's smile. He immediately wraps his lanky arms around my neck. I hug him close and whisper, "You're welcome."

8

OPAL

I wake up to excessive talking and the sound of feet shuffling. I groan, roll over, and look at my phone to see what time it is—11 a.m. I groan again and run a hand through my thick mane of red hair. My mom's painter friends come over to our house once a week at 11 a.m. Our house is the one of choice because we have a large, airy, circular room that's pretty much made for painters. I can't go downstairs and grab a cup of coffee because my mom will hear me, and her guests' attention will be drawn to me. *No thanks.*

I sit up and scroll through my phone. I open up Instagram and do the thing that no one talks about but everyone does: I type "Eli Whitlock" in the search bar. There are a few results. I eyeball each one to see if it matches. There's eli_whit, EliJAH_Whitlock, whit_lock, and eli.whitlock. I click on each, and of course, eli.whitlock is his—I can tell by his profile picture—but it's private. No one likes a private Instagram account, especially when you're trying to see that account. I could follow him, but I don't want to. That would be awkward. Or at least that's what I tell myself. I'm probably overthinking this. I go to exit out of his page, but I make a huge mistake—I accidentally hit the *follow* button. *Shit!* I hurry to unclick but actually end up unclicking it and clicking it again! I take a deep breath and slowly hit the button so it turns blue again. My heart beats rapidly. *Damn you, social media! Damn you; damn me; and damn you, sensitive phone screen.* It probably won't notify him since I undid it, right? I open up Google and type "If you follow someone on Instagram and then undo it will the other person be notified?" There are mixed answers, but it looks as if since I did it twice, I may be screwed.

Okay, it's just Instagram. No big deal, Opal.

I'm just going to hope he doesn't see it. I probably should've just left the follow request pending. It's worse now that I followed and unfollowed…twice. Oh well.

I hop off my bed and wake up my pug, Ozzie, for his walk. He glares at me in protest but ends up wobbling over to my side as I take clothes from my closet. I get dressed in a loose-fitting tee and black leggings. After brushing my teeth and pulling my hair up into a messy bun, I hook Ozzie's leash onto his collar. We walk out the front door, avoiding my mom's inquisitive friends.

I inhale the fresh air as Ozzie and I make our way to the park. Questions similar to the ones I had yesterday at lunch make their way into my head.

What happened?
Why did he have to rush out?
Is August one of his cousins?

Eli and I don't talk to each other at work much since we're in different areas of the building, so I know little about him. Going out to lunch with him the other day was a huge surprise. Maybe we'll do it again—for real next time. No interruptions. I'm going to try not to expect or assume anything. *Good luck with that, Opal.* All I know is that the way he makes me feel is unlike anything I've ever felt.

Ozzie and I get back from our walk, and my mom's friends

have dispersed. "Opal!" I hear my mom yell from the living room, she must have heard the back door.

"Yes, Mom?" I answer her while unclipping Ozzie's leash.

As I head to the living room, my mom is already walking toward me with open arms.

"Come here, honey." She brings me in for a hug. I smile and lean my head on her shoulder. Mom gives the best hugs, always.

"Hi, Mom." I kiss her on the cheek. "How was painting?"

"Great." She gives me a sweet smile and leads me into the painting room. Multiple paintings are stacked up against each other along the walls, and some are hung up around the room. My mom likes to call it "organized chaos." I sit in one of the wooden stools and cross my ankles.

I may regret what I'm about to do, but here goes. "So, there's this boy…" I start.

My mom immediately places her paintbrush down and drags her stool closer to mine.

She grabs my hands, eagerness sparking in her brown eyes, "tell me all about it."

The next morning, I awake to start my workday. As I'm getting ready, I find myself messing with my hair more than usual. *Totally NOT because of Eli.* I look at myself in the mirror and shake my head. *What are you doing?* I leave my hair the way it is. I choose my outfit: beige cardigan, white blouse, and black jeans. The most wonderful thing about working at a library is that there's no required uniform.

When I finish, I feed Ozzie and hug my mom and dad goodbye. *I almost can't fathom moving out of this house.*

When I arrive at work, Abbie winks at me, and Eli…tells his joke. I actually smile at the punchline this time. This is a good sign; maybe he didn't notice my follow/unfollow on Instagram.

I climb up the rickety steps and begin sorting through the returned books from the day before. My heart skips a beat when I look up to see Eli coming toward me. I busy myself more by shelving a couple of the books.

Eli grabs a book from the return stack and shelves it in silence before he says, "You know, Opal, it isn't a *crime* to follow someone on Instagram." He takes out his phone, and I watch him tap on it a few times. He flashes me one of his smirks that show his dimple. My stomach flutters, and my phone goes off. He doesn't take his eyes off me as I pull it out of my cardigan pocket. There's a follow notification from Instagram, and it's from him.

I take a second to follow him back. "I was just…" I start, my eyes never leaving his. I refuse to look embarrassed, even though I know my flushed skin has already given me away.

"Doing the thing that everyone does that they never admit?" He finishes my sentence.

Ha. "Yeah," I say into a giggle.

He leans against one of the bookshelves, takes out his tarot cards, and shuffles them. "So, you liked my joke this morning, huh?"

I watch him shuffle the deck with skill and speed. "I wouldn't go *that* far."

"Right. Well, I wanted to apologize again for lunch the other day. Let's reschedule?"

He spreads out the cards in his hands for me to pick one. "Um, yeah. No problem. When are you free?" I finger through the cards.

"What about next Wednesday?" He watches me as I decide on a card.

"Sure." I smile and hand him the card I chose. And once again, he gives me a reading that is eerily and *impossibly* spot on.

"Cool, Opal." He walks backward as he heads downstairs. "Try not to slide into my DMs, yeah?" His smile lights up the room as he turns around and skips down the stairs.

A smile overtakes my face as I finish shelving the books.

9

ELI

I'm parked outside the airport, waiting for my dad and uncles. August is in the passenger seat.

"Why do you keep checking your phone?" August stares out the rolled-down window, and using his mind, he picks up litter off the ground and puts it into a nearby trash can. Luckily, the airport isn't bustling with people, although that wouldn't faze August. He flaunts his ability and yet hopes no one sees it. The only reason he doesn't want anyone to notice is because he becomes easily annoyed with people's bewildered looks when they see shit floating through the air. He couldn't care less if they know it's *him* doing it—or so he claims.

"I'm checking the time." I put my phone in one of the cupholders.

"Yeah. And Instagram." August moves the last of the litter into the trash can and faces me. "Restaurant girl, huh? I'm amazed," he says nonchalantly. My cousins know that I haven't really dated since Lexi. I just haven't found anyone I can connect with on that level.

"She doesn't believe in psychics," I tell him.

I do have an attraction to Opal, but I don't know if it could ever work if she can't believe in what we do. I also need to be willing to open myself up to love again, which I'm not sure I'll ever be able to do.

"Hm" is all August answers with.

I'm about to reply when three tall, dark-haired men make their way through the airport's sliding doors. August and I step out of the car, and the three men squish us into a hug.

Clark is the first one to speak. "Felix?" Concern floods his expression.

"He's fine," I assure him as I lift his bag into the trunk. Clark nods, choosing to trust me.

We begin the drive to their house. My dad, Charles, is in the front with me, while August, Henry, and Clark are in the back. Charles, Henry, and Clark all live together with their wives. I'm not sure how they manage to make that work.

"How's the girl?" my dad asks me, staring straight ahead as the illuminated streetlights pass us by.

August coughs into a laugh, and I glare at him through the rearview mirror. Clark and Henry are looking out the passenger windows, acting as if they're not paying attention, but I know they know.

I grip the steering wheel. "There's nothing," I say to my dad, which is a half-truth. My dad and I agreed to never share our future predictions with each other. I never want to know because there's always the possibility of being influenced by the predictions. So this is his way of getting me to tell him myself. The rest of the drive is silent.

As soon as we pull up to the house on the corner of Salisbury Way, the front door to the Victorian-style house whips open. Dawson and Felix come rushing out in nothing but black sweatpants. They definitely just woke up my mom and aunts. Still, the Whitlock family is known for always being up at odd hours, so I know they're used to it. Clark, Felix, and Dawson whisper quietly among themselves. August and I help carry the luggage to the door. My dad and uncles tell us that we'll all catch up later, and August and I head back to the car.

As we start the drive home, I glance over at August and notice him rubbing his eyebrow excessively. August is the ultimate night owl. He's most energized at night—like *late* at night—and he has to be doing something. It's as if the moon's energy beckons him. This is why he chose to work as a bartender at a small dive bar not too far from our apartment.

We pull up to the apartment, and before I can even park, August jumps out of the car and sprints to the front door. I watch him cautiously as I pull the keys out of the ignition. The thing about August is that he's reliable when he needs to be. When he first started working at the bar, I was worried that he'd get into trouble while I was asleep, but so far he hasn't—at least that I've heard of, and usually, I hear of it.

I linger outside for a few minutes before stepping into the dimly lit apartment. August is already dressed for work. He gives me a dismissive, hurried wave, and I watch as he heads back out of the apartment, climbs on his sport bike, and speeds down the empty street.

What's got him in such a hurry?

I change into more comfortable clothing and fall back onto my bed. My head hits the headboard. *Shit. Ouch.* I unlock my phone and open up Instagram. *Yup, I'm gonna do it.*

I tap the message icon and search for Opal. I reach over to my nightstand and grab my sidekick in this life: my small book of jokes. I flip through the book until I find one I feel like using.

I don't overthink as I type: *Hey, Opal. What did the evil chicken lay?*

I cross my ankles, waiting for her reply.

A few minutes later, she replies: *A deviled egg. Duh.*

Damn. I shake my head. I reply: *Have you had a chance to write more?*

I watch the three little dots moving on the screen.

Sure, I've had the chance, but I haven't written.

I look up at the ceiling while I think of my next response. *This girl. Sigh.*

I text: *I hope you'll write tomorrow.*

She writes: *Don't get your hopes up. Night night.*

I run a hand down my face and toss my phone to the other side of the bed. She won't put faith in herself, but that just makes me want to put double the faith in her.

10

OPAL

You know what they say about sounding too eager when you're talking to someone? More specifically, when you're talking to someone you're into? Well, when I first heard that, I scoffed and thought, *Damn that to hell*. I mean, why should liking someone restrict us from saying or doing certain things? Well, guess what I did last night? I damned *myself* to hell and tried to sound as "not eager" as possible. Ugh. I'll let you in on a little secret: when I saw his DM, I was smiling so much that my cheeks still hurt this morning as I'm here getting ready to go to the writing group. But now, he probably thinks I'm a bitch. When I said "night night," I wasn't even going to sleep; I was scared to carry on the conversation, so I ended it. See what not "sounding too eager" got me? This is an example of why texting is difficult when it comes to letting you know how people truly feel. We can portray ourselves a million different ways through a single text message yet feel the total opposite way in real life. I could keep rambling on about our short-lived Instagram conversation last night, but the story must go on.

I tell Ozzie goodbye and give him a kiss before I start the drive to the library. Today also happens to be Wednesday; Eli and I are supposed to meet for lunch after the group session. I wonder if any of his family members will barge in today.

I pull into my usual spot at the library, exit my vehicle, and walk in through the entrance doors. When I enter the meeting room, I look around to see that I'm the only one there. *Uhhhh.*

I shrug and take a seat—a different one this time. It's against a wall, whereas the other seats aren't; I've made this choice because my back has been killing me after each session.

Maybe he cancelled the session for today, but I wasn't notified? Maybe people are sick... Oh my God. Maybe I'M sick.

My ridiculous paranoia at its finest. My paranoia is why I have a small bag of first aid items along with nail clippers, tweezers, tissues, etcetera. You name it and it's probably in my purse. I pull out a small thermometer. *Yes, I even have a thermometer.* I almost gag on it from surprise when Eli appears and leans against the open doorway that leads into the room.

He quirks an eyebrow. "What are you doing?"

He comes over to me and mockingly puts a hand on my forehead. I glare and swat it away as the thermometer beeps: 98.7. I sigh and jam it back into my purse. I grip the purse handles.

"Where is everyone?" My eyes dart around the room once more.

Eli pulls a chair up across from me and straddles it. "Oh, I cancelled today's session," he replies casually.

I give him a look as if to say *Seriously?* "Um, you could've let me know." I wave my phone in my left hand. So, he happened to let everyone know, except me. Glorious.

"Yeah, about that…"

My brows nearly reach my hairline as I wait for an explanation. My heart beats wildly.

"I thought maybe you would be able to focus better if we were alone…without the distraction of people around you."

I pause for a moment. "You didn't think to ask me first?" I cringe at my biting tone.

"Well"—he stands up from the chair and uncaps a dry-erase marker—"I knew you'd be too stubborn to agree to being here without the rest of the group, so I decided not to tell you." He turns his back to me and begins to write on the board.

My face softens at the truth in his words. Despite myself, I say, "I could just leave right now."

Oh God. I sound like a freaking five-year-old. My mom would kill me if she knew I was talking like this, but I get a thrill when Eli responds to it.

He caps the marker, with his back still facing me. "The thing is, you could. But you won't." He turns around, his arms crossed over his chest.

I scoff, give him a small smile, and tuck a strand of loose hair behind my ear. I open up my notebook and glance at the board to see the prompt. My jaw slowly drops as I read the words.

"Can we call lunch a date?"

"Is this the prompt for today, or are you serious?" I just want to hear it from his mouth.

He rolls his eyes. "I mean, if this is something you think you can write about, then sure, it's a prompt." He flashes me a knowing smile, his dimple making an appearance.

"It's a date." I distract myself by scribbling on a blank page. When I look up at him, he claps his hands and begins erasing the board. He uncaps his marker again and writes a new word.

"Psychics"

11

ELI

I watch her reaction as she peers up at the word on the board. I wonder what she'll write about *this* topic, if she'll even write anything at all.

She laughs. "Is this your way of seeing how I *really* feel about psychics?" She gives me a pointed look.

I shrug. She's right. "Write about why you don't believe," I tell her.

She rests her chin on her knuckles as if pondering what to write about. She begins scribbling, and she pauses to look up at me.

"Please don't stare." She glares at me. I hold my hands up in surrender and open up my phone to find seventy-three unread texts. *The group chat.* August, Dawson, Felix and I are all in a group chat, and right now it looks as if August and Dawson are arguing about which essential oil is best for sleep. I didn't realize how in depth two people could go when discussing oil scents. *Only my cousins.*

I glance through the texts quickly, and I sigh in relief as the notification alerts go away. There are some people—August—

who have like thirty thousand unread emails. I would go into cardiac arrest if I had that many.

"Done," Opal announces cheerfully. I walk over to her, and she holds up a hand to stop me.

"Uh-uh...no. You aren't reading what I wrote until you tell me everything about your fascination with psychics and tarot cards."

I scratch the back of my neck and angle my head toward the door. I wasn't going to read what she wrote. "Let's take a walk."

Opal starts packing up her things. "We're still going to get something to eat, right?"

A chuckle escapes me. "Yes."

She nods and shoulders her purse. I lead her outside, and we start walking in the direction of downtown. She stuffs her hands into her coat pockets, and I look down at the cracked sidewalk, figuring out where the hell to start. She waits patiently while I gather my thoughts.

"So...my dad and his two brothers have psychic abilities. It's genetic." I look down at Opal, and she nods slightly, encouraging me to continue. "My dad and I have what's called clairsentience, which allows us to acquire knowledge by means of feeling. So, we're in tune with other people's feelings. This is why tarot cards work well for us, because we can correlate what the card means to what someone is feeling." I pause, but she remains silent.

She notices my pause. "I just don't want to ask questions until you're finished, and I don't want my skepticism to discourage you." She looks up at me with a hint of wonder in her eyes.

I breathe in and continue. "So, August, the one who interrupted our lunch, is one of my cousins. He's nineteen. Him and his father, Henry, have the ability of telekinesis... I bet I don't have to explain that one."

She lets out a breathy laugh. "You're correct."

I feel something hanging off her words; it's as if she wants to say something else but is holding back. The only person I've told before is Lexi, but I try not to remember how she reacted. It's not fair for me to compare her reaction to Opal's.

"Last but not least, my twin cousins, Felix and Dawson, have different abilities. Felix is a psychic medium like his dad, Clark. A psychic medium is someone who has the ability to speak to the dead. Dawson is able to see events that happen in the future, like our grandpa."

Okay, I think it's time to stop for now. I want to make sure she has time to process everything. This might scare her away. I hope with everything in me that this doesn't happen. I wait for her response.

Her eyebrows are bunched together; she's in deep thought. Thinking can either be good or bad. I refuse to use my ability on her. It's an invasion of privacy if I don't have approval.

Right on cue, she says, "Don't get in my head."

I meet her eyes. "I would never do that...and I thought you didn't believe." My words are sincere.

We hold each other's stare for a moment. She opens her mouth to speak and then closes it. When she opens it again, I'm not expecting what comes out.

"Why would you make up something like this? I mean, like I explained to you earlier, I only didn't believe in it because I didn't understand it. But...somehow, it feels different now that you've told me."

I nod. "Well, don't be afraid to ask questions. I hope this doesn't scare you away, because I was looking forward to our date."

"I'm still here, aren't I?" She winks. I laugh.

I stop in front of a Japanese restaurant and point at the entrance. "You like sushi?"

"Yes!" She pulls open the door enthusiastically, and I follow her inside. When we're seated, she reaches into her purse, rips out a page from her notebook, and slides it to me with a smirk.

I slide the paper closer to me, and I feel the heat rising from my neck as I read what's written. It's what she wrote at the library:

"Topic: Psychic

I'm interested in you, so spit out what you have to say about psychics before I say something close-minded and cynical and skeptical-y."

12

OPAL

So, psychics. Of course, a guy that I'm actually interested in is a damn psychic, and on top of that, he has a whole family of them! I have some tact, okay. I can be rude, brash, and cynical, but I was starting to get the feeling that the psychic stuff meant something to him, so I put my pride aside and let him explain, as I would do for my parents or Abbie. I was actually surprised at what I wrote at the library.

I thought, *What would Abbie do?* So, I channeled my best friend and told the person I like how I feel. I'm just tired of skipping around things when it comes to feelings. I'm twenty-three, not fifteen…you know? I felt so stupid over the whole Instagram thing; it was time to step it up.

This is new territory for me. I haven't blushed from the attention of a guy since I was…fifteen. Ha.

After he reads what's on the page, his brown eyes meet my green, and I see the blush creeping up his neck. Abbie kept saying that all of his stupid jokes and card readings meant he was into me, but I just didn't believe her. But now, seeing the way he looks at me, I might just owe her a phone call later. I never in a million trillion years thought I'd be into a psychic; better yet, I never thought I'd actually believe someone who said they were one. But there's something about Eli that is undeniably genuine, and he deserves the benefit of the doubt.

He clears his throat. "You know...you're only the second person I've told in detail about me and my family." His eyes flash with an intensity I've never seen.

I might regret this, but I say softly, "Who was the first?"

He fiddles with the white wrapping on his chopsticks.

"You don't need to—"

"Her name was Lexi," he blurts.

Oh. Oh God. I feel like this is about to get emotional, and I cringe internally. Emotion and I don't get along well. But, again, I give Eli the benefit of the doubt. This brown-eyed psychic is beginning to be an exception to all of my rules.

After he tells me about Lexi, I look down at my hands and feel a lump creeping up my throat. I shove it down. *Crying won't help anything, Opal.*

I exhale. "I am so sorry, Eli. Thank you for sharing that with me."

I mean, what do I say to that? What *should* I say to that?

I reach across the small table and rest my hand on his arm. I don't even know if comfort is what he needs.

"Thank you." Tears begin to well in his eyes. I offer him a small smile. He sniffs and looks around the restaurant as if to make sure no one saw. He shouldn't be ashamed to cry, although I know I'd be embarrassed too. Thankfully, the restaurant isn't busy. Only one other table is occupied—one of the perks of living in a small town.

While we wait for our food, I continue to process what he told me on the walk there. I don't want to ask him questions about Lexi yet. So, I let my mind wander until he asks me about writing. *Ugh. Writing.*

A teasing smile plays on his lips as if he knows I get irritated when he brings it up. It's not really that; it's just frustrating that I don't have anything cool to say.

Since I was little, I've felt a tug—a tug telling me to write. It's aggravating to have this a tug of need throughout your life but not get anything out of it. It's like an itch that desperately needs to be scratched. I keep this information to myself.

I'm relieved when our food comes, as I can focus on eating instead of writing.

"So, where do you get all of your jokes?" I ask, playing with my food. This better be good.

"A book of jokes." I lift up my arms as if to say *What the hell?* But before I can express my disgust, he continues, "I know, I know. I'm so lame for that. I wish I could tell you that I make them up." A smile pulls at his lips.

"Damn. I was hoping for something good. You're a fraud!"

The other couple in the restaurant turns to look at us with curious eyes, and when Eli starts to laugh, I join in, nearly choking on my water.

I'm drowning in the depths of Eli Whitlock, and I don't foresee myself coming up for air.

13

OPAL

"365" by Zedd and Katy Perry blares over the speakers as Abbie; her girlfriend, Leah; and I enter The Black Jacket, a small dive bar in town. Abbie pulls me by the arm over to the leather barstools. We take our seats, and a tall guy with a buzz cut takes our order. I wasn't enthusiastic about coming tonight, but Abbie insisted, and they do have the best gin and tonic.

The emotions from my date with Eli have consumed me. Abbie shimmies her shoulders to the music as we wait for our drinks. I rest my elbows on the bar and blow a strand of hair from my face.

Leah rests a hand on my arm. "What's up with you tonight?" she prods gently.

Abbie comes up behind Leah and rests her head on her shoulder. They start swaying to the music.

"You know, she had a *date* earlier." Abbie wiggles her eyebrows and flashes a bright smile. I called Abbie after the date and told her...well, the bare minimum. I didn't want to tell her about Eli's family of psychics or Lexi. It's not my place.

I groan and wave my hand, dismissing the conversation. Leah squeezes my shoulder in comfort, and I welcome it. I give her and Abbie a warm smile. I'm trying not to be "Broody Bernice," as Abbie calls me whenever I get into a mood. You know, I say I'm not into emotions, but then why do I let them take over? Abbie kisses my cheek, and she and Leah twirl their way onto the dance floor.

I'm staring at my hands when I hear a glass hit the bar. I glance up to find my order of gin and tonic, but when I lift myself up onto the stool to take a sip...Oh *shit*.

August fucking Whitlock is smiling down at me. The blood drains from my face.

"Hi, Opie." He winks. *He did not just call me "Opie."*

"Please don't ever call me that," I retort with a glare.

August wipes a glass clean with a dish towel as he continues to stare at me. "Sorry!" He smirks.

"You know, I'm sorry, okay? It's just..." My phone chimes, stopping me mid-sentence. It's an Instagram notification from Eli. I'm about to open up the message to reply when my phone leaves my hands and floats across the bar into August's large hand. *So, this is how it's going to be. And I just saw my phone float...* I shake my head to rid my mind of the thought.

"Give it back." I reach over the bar and try to snatch my phone back, but I just end up spilling my drink across the wooden counter. August is paying me no mind as he begins typing. Typing?! Ooooh, no. Absolutely not.

An annoying smile overtakes his face as he types.

"August. Give. It. Back." God, I feel like I'm talking to a child. I feel my armpits start to sweat, and I try to remember whether I put on deodorant.

"Sheesh! Fine." August hands my phone back, and I grab it. He resumes cleaning the glass and watches me while I hurriedly check what damage he has done. Instead of finding my Instagram DMs open, I find the Notes app open with a link: "100 Writing Prompts for Beginners."

Through all of my Google searching regarding writing, I haven't seen a website with this many prompts. I look up at him in awe, not sure how to react since I assumed the worst when he took my phone. He just smiles, and I don't miss the genuine look in his eye as he refills my drink. I assume Eli told him about me and the fact that I'm in his writing group. The thought causes my heart to flutter.

I offer him a soft smile, and I open Instagram again to reply to Eli.

Him: *What are you doing?*

Me: *At a dive bar with Abbie and her girlfriend. I didn't know August worked here.*

The three dots instantly appear on the screen, and then they disappear. I frown at the screen. August raises a brow at me when I hear Abbie and Leah scream my name, beckoning me to dance. August laughs softly before he goes to help someone who just entered the bar. I take my gin and tonic with me. I feel a bit of liquid courage come over me as I take another sip from the half-empty glass. I sway to the beat beside Abbie and Leah. We raise our hands above our heads, screaming and laughing.

I'm finishing off my drink when I feel a hand on my shoulder. I lock eyes with Abbie, and a small smile plays on her lips. I slowly turn around to find Eli staring down at me.

I'd be what you call a "lightweight." I squint. "What are you doing here?"

He looks at Abbie and Leah as if asking for their permission to pull me away. They give him small nods and continue dancing. Eli gently guides me away from the small dance floor.

"Are you okay?" He eyes the bar, looking for August, I assume.

"Yes... Why wouldn't I be?" I hold up my glass.

"Because"—he pins his gaze on August, who is talking to someone at the bar—"of him." I notice a slight bite in his tone.

"He didn't do anything," I assure Eli. "What's your problem?" I mean, it's kind of obvious that there's some tension between the two cousins, but what does that have to do with me?

"Nothing." Eli finally tears his eyes away from August, but not before scowling at him. His eyes meet mine, and his jaw twitches. "Hey, do you want to get outta here? It's the twins' birthday, and we're having a party at my apartment."

"Uh, sure. Let me clear it with Abbie and Leah first."

He gives me a half smile and nods.

"Date with the psychic, huh?" Abbie waggles her eyebrows. Leah looks up at me with raised brows.

I roll my eyes. "No. Well, maybe. I don't know... He's taking me to his cousins' birthday party."

"Oh my God. Totally a date!" Abbie screams excitedly. She playfully slaps my ass. "Have fun!"

I roll my eyes again, but I can't help but smile. I turn around to find Eli behind the bar; it looks as if he and August are in a staring contest. They're probably doing their telepathy thing. I walk over to the bar and watch them. August is the first one to break eye contact.

"Hey again, Opie!" August says with a jovial grin. Now it's Eli's turn to roll his eyes. I glare at August as Eli comes around the bar and leads me out the door.

14

ELI

Dawson and Felix's birthdays are always low-key. Although they have many friends, they prefer to celebrate holidays with family only. I asked them ahead of time if it would be okay to bring Opal; surprisingly, they agreed.

We show up to my apartment, and I introduce Opal to my dad and uncles and then to my mom and aunts. They all give us soft smiles. My uncles are in the kitchen making their famous cupcakes. They're still the best ones I've had to this day; every year, they make them for my cousins and me for our birthdays.

I'm not even sure how we all fit in the apartment. My dad and uncles are crowded into the small kitchen, and my mom and aunts are spread out along the small kitchen island, watching them at work. Dawson and Felix are on the couch, whispering quietly to each other.

I intertwine my fingers with Opal's as we walk over to the couch. She looks down at her feet, a blush blooming furiously on her cheeks. She tightens her hold on my hand. *She's so cute.*

Dawson and Felix must hear us approaching because they whip their heads toward us. A warm smile overtakes Felix's face, while Dawson greets us with a soft smile.

"Guys, this is Opal." She gives them a small wave. "Happy Birthday," she says with a tentative smile.

Thanks!" Dawson and Felix say at the same time. Dawson nudges Felix's shoulder playfully.

"Happy birth—" I start, but an overwhelming vibrating pain shoots through my head. I smack a hand to my head and stumble back.

"Eli?" Opal asks, confusion and worry in her voice. Dawson and Felix are at my side immediately. Dawson screams for my dad. I try to talk, but nothing comes out. My vision becomes blurry as I see my mom carefully pulling Opal aside. My dad crouches next to me and holds my shoulder. I hear the mix of my cousins screaming and my uncles talking hurriedly.

First, my hearing vanishes.

Then, blackness overtakes me.

My eyes open slowly. I'm lying faceup on a table. The pain in my head seems to have gone.

Where the fuck am I? Where's Opal?

The first thing I see is the familiar green wooden ceiling of my family's house. I breathe a sigh of relief. As my sense of feeling returns, I notice a slight pressure on my forehead. I slowly raise my hand to my forehead, and I feel a cottony fabric.

Before I can decipher exactly what it is, August yells, "HE'S UP!"

I wince at the loud sound. I hear sets of footsteps hurrying toward me.

"Eli?" I hear my dad's voice in my ear. I blink a couple of times and turn my head slightly. My dad smiles softly at me, relief coating his features.

"What happened?" My voice is thick. My dad and Uncle Clark exchange glances.

Oh God... Is it bad? I don't have the energy to demand answers, so I just lie there.

"So, you're in love," August says matter-of-factly. I look around the table and see my dad and uncles shoot withering glares at August.

"What?" I'm not sure what is going on at all, and I don't like it. *And why is August even here? Isn't he supposed to be at work?* I grunt at all the questions entering my mind at warp speed.

"Just relax," Charles coaxes.

"Can I get up?" I ask, annoyed. When no one answers, I roll my wrists and rise from the table. My shirt is sweaty and sticks to me. A fresh shirt flies down on my lap, courtesy of August. I chuck the sweaty shirt at August, but he stops it in midair, cringes, and moves it into the nearest laundry basket.

I feel my forehead again and realize that the fabric is a headband. I take the hot headband off my head and hold it in my hands. The potent scents of patchouli and orange surround me. I crinkle my nose and then realize that the combination isn't bad.

"Can someone please tell me what's happening?" I twirl the black headband around my wrist.

"I told yo—" August begins, but my dad holds up a hand to stop him. August shrugs and shoves his hands into his jacket pockets. Clark gingerly takes the headband from my hand and sets it down on the counter behind him. My palms begin to sweat as I look to my dad for answers.

"Eli, son, there's something you need to know...something that we've...*I've* waited to tell you, and you'll find out the reason I've waited." My dad's voice is calming, but his words don't calm me down. I have no problem being calm when it comes to my family's problems, but when it comes to my own, forget it.

I glance over at August, who is now juggling his mother's expensive glass figurines in midair while everyone is distracted. I refocus my attention on my father.

"You ever wondered why we all married so fast?" My father gestures to my uncles. My parents got married within only two months of meeting, while my aunts and

uncles got married just one month after their first dates.

"I guess..."

"Well, when we all met our wives, we felt pain similar to what you felt today. This thing runs in the Whitlock family. Your grandfather knew how to treat it because it happened to him, his father, and so on. That's why you woke up with a headband covered in patchouli and orange oils. It helps relieve the pain. But don't worry; it only happens once in a lifetime." My father's tone is nonchalant.

"*What* happens?" I am losing patience.

He rests a comforting hand on my shoulder, and I brace myself for what will come next.

"You meet your soulmate."

I put two and two together. Opal is my soulmate? What? I mean, do I feel an attraction toward her? Sure. But *soulmate*? It would make sense that this is the first time in ten years that I've felt a strong connection with a woman. I brace my palms on the table and look down at my feet. What if she doesn't want this?

"What if she doesn't feel the same way?" I ask the room full of men who are far more knowledgeable than I am.

"Oh, she will. It wouldn't happen if she didn't," Clark tells me.

I nod to myself. "And why does *he* know?" I jut my chin toward August, who places the figurines back in their spots.

"He knows because we knew that he wouldn't be as...*caring* about the situation as you or your other cousins would. So we knew from the beginning that when it did happen to you, we'd clue August in on it," Clark explains.

"Okay..." I can't deny that August wouldn't be as affected by this. He is usually indifferent when it comes to his love life; it's something I will never understand.

"Where do I go from here?" I tighten my grip on the table.

"Just go about life how you usually would," my dad says.

"And what about telling Opal?" I cringe at the thought. I *just* let her into my psychic world, and now *this*?

My dad gives me a pointed look. "That is entirely up to you."

15

OPAL

I can't get what happened the other day out of my head. One minute, I was being introduced to Eli's cousins, and the next, I was being ushered out of his apartment by his mother. Eli and I haven't spoken much, except for the necessary communication at work. He hasn't even told any jokes, which I've honestly grown to miss even though it's been only three days. I've been dying to ask him what went down, but I've come to the conclusion that it would be better if he brought it up himself. If I deserve to know, he will tell me. I must really like him, because with anyone else, I would demand answers. My hesitation could be because I'm still processing that he and his family are actual psychics. I push down my thoughts as I walk through the library's sliding doors.

As I approach the meeting room, I'm relieved to see that the regular attendants are present. I take my usual seat and pull out my notebook and pen from my purse. Eli greets the class and then glances at me. I give him a small smile. He turns away from me and begins writing our one-word prompt on the whiteboard:

"Soulmates"

I scoff—more loudly than I meant to since a couple of people look at me. *Soulmates? Really, Eli?*

I don't think soulmates exists. It's total romantic disillusionment. I mean, there's no *one* person who is right for you; there are probably many. There are seven billion people in this world.

I shake my head as I begin writing furiously. This is going to sound more like a rant. But, hey, I'm writing, right?

I finish and cap my pen. I look around the room to see people still writing. Most of them are probably writing about these beautiful nonexistent romances. I pick at my nails while I wait. Eli strides over to me. *Shit.* I continue picking at my extremely interesting nails.

"Hey, Opal?" he whispers.

"Yes?" I reply softly, not meeting his gaze. A joke?

"How does it feel?"

"What do you mean? My eyes meet his, and his voice caresses my skin.

"To be at the forefront of all of my thoughts." His mouth is so close to my ear that I can feel his warm breath against my tingling skin.

He backs away, leaving me in a daze. I stubbornly shake it off. No man is going to put Opal O'Connell in a trance.

I watch him as he makes his way to the front of the room and says goodbye to everyone. It's as if my ass is glued to the seat, because I don't move to the exit with the rest of them.

As he comes over to me again, I don't shy away from checking him out. The confident energy in the way he walks, the way his eyebrows come together as if he's thinking hard about something... Okay, maybe I *am* in a trance. I revel in it for the first time in my life. He flashes me a smile, his dimple making an appearance, and motions for me to stand. So I do and shoulder my purse. He nods toward the door, and I follow him out.

Is this when he tells me what happened?

I have to run a little to keep up with his long strides as we make our way down the street.

"Can I talk to you about something? About what happened last night?" he asks tentatively.

Yes! I had a feeling he would come around to telling me. Well, I was hoping so anyway.

"Of course," I tell him. His eyes darken slightly. Okay... Should I be worried?

So, he tells me. About the headband, about waking up on a table surrounded by his father and uncles, and then...about the soulmate part. Is this some kind of joke? This is not at all what I was expecting.

"Is this some kind of joke?" I take out my notebook, rip out the page I wrote about soulmates, and shove it against his chest. "Want to know what I think? Read that."

"Opal, I—"

I hold up a hand to stop him. "I haven't even processed the fact that you're an actual psychic, and now you're trying to tell me I'm your soulmate? ME? C'mon, Eli. Nice move using that as our prompt today."

"You're not listening," he tries to explain. I back up a step, and he moves forward a step.

I raise both of my hands. "I should go... I'm sorry," I mumble.

"OPAL!" he yells as I turn around and make my way down the street in a hurry to get away from the conversation...to get away from *him*.

"He said WHAT?" Abbie is bewildered, and I'm glad I'm not the only one. But then she breaks out into a big smile. *Or not.*

"No, Abbie, this isn't good. I've never been in love... Shit, I've never been in *like*, and now Eli Whitlock is trying to tell me that I'm his soulmate?" I plop down onto my bed.

She lies down next to me, props her elbow up, and rests her head in her hand.

"Okay, Op, don't get mad...but maybe you're just overwhelmed with the whole psychic thing...and your feelings for him."

I want to glare at her, but I think better of it because she's right.

"What do I do?" I mumble into my pillow.

Abbie rubs my back soothingly. "Talk to him."

"Ugh. It's always *talking*."

She responds with a light laugh.

What am I going to tell my parents? *Oh, yeah... There's this guy, and he's a psychic and from a whole family of psychics, and, oh yeah, he says he's my soulmate.* I shake my head while I spit toothpaste into the sink. Work is going to be super awkward. I groan at the thought. I throw my hair up in a ponytail and head to the kitchen for breakfast.

"Hi, honey," my dad says. He's sitting at the kitchen table studying a blueprint of one of the properties he designs.

"Hi, Dad. Where's Mom?" I look around the kitchen.

"Oh, she had to go into work early again." He rolls his eyes. I roll mine too. Mom's work always makes her go in early. She works at a local florist, and they're always slammed. I still don't like the way they treat her. I think back to the card reading Eli gave me in relation to that.

I place a coffee cup under the Keurig and press START. As the coffee flows out, I pop two slices of bread into the toaster. I feel my dad's gaze on my back.

"You okay?" he asks, still studying his blueprint.

I sigh quietly. "Yes, Dad. Thanks for asking." I look back to see him nodding to himself. *Yeah, he knows something's up.*

I take the toast out of the toaster, spread some peanut butter on it, and gulp down the coffee. I place the coffee cup in the sink and head back to my bedroom to grab my stuff. I say goodbye to Daddy and Ozzie before heading out the door.

I arrive at work and internally cringe when I spot Eli helping a customer. I was kind of hoping he wouldn't be there, but he's no coward. Maybe it'll be like when we didn't talk to each other after the incident at his apartment, but I'd be fooling myself if I said I wanted it to go the same way.

I climb the steps to my little library and begin to sort through books. My eyes widen as I hear footsteps coming up the stairs. I start mindlessly organizing the paperwork sprawled across my desk when Eli stops in front of me. I slowly look up. I feel my face heating as he looks down at me.

"Hey, Opal." His voice is soft.

I give him a half-assed smile and carry an armful of books to the shelves. He follows me.

"Why can't you go into the world's largest library?" he asks. Okay, this one's definitely a joke. When I stubbornly refuse to reply, he continues. "Because it's always overbooked!"

When I don't laugh, he sighs. "Look, Opal. I don't want it to be this way between us. I know I've given you a lot of information in the past week or so. I really want to keep helping you with your writing, but if you don't want to come to the group anymore, I would understand. I know I'm probably overwhelming you." He stops and waits for my reply. I feel a tug in my chest when I think about what happened to his ex, Lexi, and how he also revealed himself to her, however not that she was his soulmate.

Okay, stop being stubborn, Opal. "Yes, Eli. I am overwhelmed.

Look, I like you, I do. It's just that I wasn't expecting this much… and I'm not the best with emotional stuff. If you read the note I gave you, you would know how I feel about soulmates."

He looks at me, his eyes full of earnest. "I didn't read it."

I take a breath. "Well, it explains how I don't believe in soulmates."

Eli shifts uncomfortably. "Oh" is his only reply. I continue to shelve books, trying to figure out what to say.

"But maybe we can try something out," I tell him casually as he follows me down the line of bookshelves.

"How about…let me take you out on another date?"

I can sense that he's trying to keep the eagerness out of his voice. "Will there be interrupting cousins?" I feel a smile playing on my lips.

"I'll make sure that there's not." He rubs the back of his neck.

"Okay, then." I know that every part of me wants to give him a chance. Who knows? Maybe I'll start believing in the whole soulmate thing… Highly doubtful, though.

"Okay… Tomorrow after work?" His eyes are gleaming with hope when I turn to look at him.

I shelve the last of the books. "Sure."

16

ELI

My shift ended two hours ago, and Opal is still at work. I pace in the living room of the apartment. Maybe I'm letting this whole soulmate thing get to my head. I mean, there's a sort of pressure that comes with being told that someone is your soulmate when you haven't even established a real relationship with them. I trust my uncles, especially since they've all gone through it themselves. I want it to be natural with Opal. I don't want her to think I want to be with her just because I found out that she's my so-called soulmate. Maybe I shouldn't have even brought it up to her this soon. Frustrated, I run a hand through my hair.

August strides into the room, his nonchalant aura as irritating as always. "What are you doing?"

I wave a hand, dismissing his question. In truth, I'm thinking of my date with Opal and the fact that I have to pick her up in twenty minutes. *I need this to be right.*

A pillow hits me in the head. I turn to glare at August, who now has his arms crossed over his bare chest.

"Look, I know you're worried about Opal, but she'll come around." August shrugs.

I don't ask how he knows about Opal's hesitation. August knows me better than anyone, and I know that my body language is giving everything away. I give him a lot of shit, but he has a keen eye.

I check the time on my phone and grab my wallet from the coffee table. "Gotta go." August gives me an all-knowing smirk. I shake my head as I slam the front door behind me.

When I open the door to Beans N' Books, Abbie is putting bags of coffee beans away on shelves, and Opal is leaning against the bar. They're laughing. I approach them and clear my throat. Abbie raises a brow at me while Opal adjusts her purse strap.

"Hey, Eli. Let's go," Opal says.

I raise a brow back at Abbie and lead Opal out the door.

"So, where are we going?" Opal asks, as I open the passenger door for her. She gives a small smile in thanks.

"It's a surprise," I tell her with a wink. She nods in response and fiddles with her fingernails.

I climb into the driver's seat and start the car. "So, I apologize for springing that on you."

"Thanks… It just took me by surprise, naturally." She gazes out the window. I connect my phone to Bluetooth, and the Goo Goo Dolls blares through the speakers.

Opal looks at me and beams. "You like them?" Her voice is filled with excitement.

"Yeah. Who doesn't?" I turn the volume up a bit more and start to drive.

When we pull up to the beach, I inhale the ocean air. I look over and see Opal doing the same.

She lets out a small laugh. "You come to the beach often?" she asks as she takes her shoes off.

"Yes. I come here for calm because my cousins can be a lot sometimes." I slip my own shoes off.

I take our shoes and throw them in the trunk. She nods in understanding and then takes off toward the water in a full-on sprint. I let out a surprised laugh. I run to catch up to her. As the freezing water nips at her ankles, she spins around, tilts her head back, and smiles. Her red hair spins around her. She doesn't let the cold air or frigid water distract her. I pause and just admire her.

"You're beautiful!" I say from my spot about ten feet from her. She stops twirling and faces me. Her hair cascades down her shoulders.

She pauses and then motions toward the water. "Come on!"

I run, swiftly pick her up in my arms, and carry her out into the water.

"Put me down!" She laughs while hitting my shoulder. I set her down gently, and she splashes me.

"The betrayal." I smirk and splash her back. She giggles and ties her hair up. "I've never seen you so happy," I blurt.

She gives me a soft smile. "You don't know me that well, do you?" I guess she's right. "So, Eli, tell me what I'm feeling. Work your magic on me."

I raise my eyebrows as if to ask if she's sure. She waves me on. The water laps at my knees as I close my eyes. As soon as I do, she pushes me. She laughs loudly as I jump up and push my now-wet hair out of my eyes. I shiver.

"The betrayal...*again*. What am I going to do with you?" I take a step closer to her and gently brush a strand of her hair away from her face.

"Let's try our hand at seeing how things work out." Her eyes shine as she looks at me.

I pull her in close, and her chin rises slightly. "Is this okay?" I whisper against her lips.

"Yes," she whispers back.

I press my lips to hers.

I kiss her.
I kiss her gently so she knows I'll take care of her.
I kiss her slowly so I can savor this moment with her.
I kiss her with meaning so she knows I want this. I want *us*.
I kiss her hoping she does too.

17

OPAL

When we break the kiss, I bring a hand to my lips. Our faces are still inches apart. "That...was my first kiss," I confess to Eli. He doesn't look shocked like I expect him to.

"How'd I do?" A smile plays at his lips, causing his dimple to make its usual appearance.

I laugh and playfully punch him in the shoulder. It's as if realization has slapped me in the face. I'm happy. Being around Eli makes me happy. It's as if a weight is lifted off me every time we're together. I want him in my life. I *need* him in my life. *Abbie is going to give me soooo much shit later!* She's the one who is always telling me that I'm so closed off. It's time for me to open myself up. All of this is new to me—the psychics...the *romance*. But I'm ready to jump in headfirst with Eli Whitlock.

"What's on your mind?" Eli asks. He could easily figure out what I'm feeling with his psychic superpowers, but it seems he doesn't.

"I want to be with you," I tell him. "No more stubbornness, no more this, no more that. I want you. I want to try this out with you."

His smile overtakes his face as he scoops me up and twirls

me around. I peck his cheek, and he kisses me again with me in his arms.

After another hour at the beach, we're both soaked and shivering.

"Hot chocolate?" Eli asks.

"YES!" I scream, wringing my hair out while we walk back to his car.

He pulls into a hut-sized drive-up coffee shop and orders two hot chocolates. We then pull up to a parking spot that overlooks the beach.

"So, how come you've never been kissed?"

I knew this was coming. I answer honestly. "I just...haven't found the right one. I usually push people away."

He nods to himself, seeming not to judge me. "Opal... I hope I never make you feel like you have to push me away. Please always let me know if I overstep any boundaries or make you feel uncomfortable in any way." He looks at me earnestly. His eyes tell me that he means every word.

I nod, take a big sip of my hot chocolate, and nervously tuck a piece of hair behind my ear. "No one's ever said anything like that to me," I say quietly, almost to myself.

He presses a warm kiss to my temple, and we watch the sunset in blissful silence.

18

OPAL

I PULL MY SPARKLY BABY-BLUE SKIRT DOWN SO IT'S NOT RIDING UP my ass. I douse my now larger-than-life hair with more hairspray. Apparently, the Whitlock cousins host a Halloween party every year. Eli and I, as cliché as it is, are going as a couple from the 80s. Eli invited Abbie, who's getting ready at Leah's house, and Eli is beside me, putting a handful of gel in his hair.

"I don't think you need that much." I turn up my nose at the amount of gel in his palm.

"You could say that about your hairspray," he retorts. Okay, he has a point.

I put the cap back on the hairspray and apply deep-red lipstick to my full lips.

When we arrive at the abandoned warehouse, it's already packed with people.

I see Abbie and Leah sitting in front of the neon purple bar. I tug on Eli's arm and lead him to my friends.

"Nice party, Whitlock!" Leah takes a sip of her green drink. Abbie kisses my cheek.

"Oh, it's mostly August's doing," Eli replies as he looks around the room.

"That would be me!" August pops up from behind the bar. Abbie and Leah giggle as Eli and I glare at the blond-haired psychic.

"Tough crowd... Well, some of you." He winks at Abbie and Leah as he pours a drink.

"Oh! Look, Felix! It's the *soulmates* in the flesh," Dawson slurs as Felix wraps an arm around his waist to hold him up.

Felix shoots Eli an apologetic smile. "I tried to stop him," he whispers.

Why is he whispering?

Eli snatches the beer away from Dawson and slams it down on the bar. *Oh...*

"Felix, take him home...now. Please." Eli glares at Dawson. Felix mumbles something in Dawson's ear, and they hobble toward the doors.

Eli wraps a loving arm around my shoulders and pulls me close. Maybe I can get used to this soulmate thing.

"What do ya have, hairspray?" August turns to me. I roll my eyes and order water.

"Laaaame," August drawls as he fills a cup with water. "I know Mr. Protective Cousin isn't going to have anything." He places the water on the counter.

"You're right about that. Come on, Opal. I want to show you something," Eli says.

Both Abbie and Leah blow me a kiss before Eli takes my hand and leads me out of the room.

Okay, maybe I did apply too much hairspray, because now my scalp is starting to itch. Eli takes me up a flight of stairs at the back of the warehouse. The metal stairs echo as we climb them.

Eli reaches into his back pocket and pulls out a set of keys. "Close your eyes."

I do. I don't usually like surprises, but my stomach flutters in excitement as I hear a lock turn. Eli pulls my hand, and I feel the night breeze caress my face. Okay...we're outside...

"Open."

I do. Tears start to prick my eyes as I look around. We're on a balcony. Fairy lights hang from the awning like long icicles, and at the end of each hangs a slip of paper. Orange roses, my favorite flower, adorn the balcony railing.

"Eli, I...wow. Thank you. I've never been surprised like this." I wipe my wet cheeks.

He smiles and kisses my cheek. "Open the first note." He points to the closest slip of paper dangling in front of us.

I give him a look as I detach the note from the lights. With shaking hands, I open it.

I see one word: "My."

I give Eli a puzzled look. He nods, prompting me to open the second note. I do. It reads "Love." I giggle to myself as I reach for the third note. The lights sway as I pluck it off. It reads "For."

"My Love For... "

The fourth one reads "You."

The fifth one reads "Is."

I carefully open the sixth and last note. It reads "OTHERWORLDLY."

"My Love For You Is Otherworldly."

I instantly wrap my arms around Eli's neck.

"I love you, Opal."

"I love you too, Eli."

I've never been so sure of anything.

He brings me in closer to him and pulls a small remote from his pocket. He laughs softly into my hair. I grin and nuzzle into him.

I let out a small gasp as "Without You Here" by the Goo Goo Dolls begins playing.

He takes my hand in his, and we dance.
And we dance.

19
―――
OPAL

One month later

I'm feeling confident for the first time since I set foot in *Meeting Room 1*. I've had an extra skip in my step since Eli told me he loved me.

Eli gives me a knowing look as I take my usual seat, and he writes the weekly prompt on the board.

Screw the prompt.

Ever since that night, I've been itching to write—like *actually* write—and it feels so good to finally be doing it. Two weeks ago, I came up with an idea, and I've decided to run with it. No more crazy cat lady stories, it's time for something real. For the first time, looking around the room at the other writers gives me a sense of hope, not envy.

Eli made me believe that this creativity has been inside of me all along. It was like a fire that was left to embers, waiting to be ignited once and for all.

I flip through pages in my notebook that I never thought I would fill and when I make it to a fresh page, I begin to write furiously. Is this what inspiration feels like?

My inspiration came unexpectedly.

At the hands of love.

At the hands of Eli Whitlock.

I pause and scribble the title on one of the page's side margins: *Otherworldly.*

20

ELI

I wake to the sharp sound of glass shattering. I sit up, alert. It must be around dawn. *What the hell was that?*

I quickly make my way to the living room to see August come around the corner of the hallway that leads to his bedroom, panic lines his features.

I glance at him and put a finger to my lips. August nods and glances around the room, his usually calm expression now grim.

August suddenlyshoves me behind him as a man dressed in black comes into view from behind the couch that is next to the window. I grab his arm in an attempt to pull him behind me, but he yanks it away.

"If you don't stay behind me, I swear to the Universe." His tone has a biting edge I've never heard before.

The man is holding a knife, and a mask covers his face, concealing his identity.

I ignore August, letting him stay in front of me, but I move closer to him. "Who the fuck are you?" I sneer.

"Cute. Cousins protecting each other." The man says.

"He asked you a question," August growls, his body visibly tensing.

"Oh, you're probably wondering why you can't use your precious telekinesis to fling this knife out of my hand… Well, let me tell you." The intruder saunters over to a chair and straddles it. The knife dangles eerily from his fingers. "I spoke to a witch, and he put a kind of magical shield on this knife, if you will. I didn't think it would work, but hey."

Our family knows a family of witches… the Undergroves… but it couldn't have been them, could it?

"What do you want?" I grit out.

The man lets out a sinister laugh. "Well, I'm here for your uncles. They're the reason my wife divorced me. THE REASON MY LIFE ENDED!" he screams, standing up straighter suddenly.

He continues, "Your uncles told my wife about how she needed to focus on her career… and Ophelia took that to heart, and she left me. Every fucking day after that reading, all she would talk about is *her career that, her career this*. It consumed her. Your uncles did that to her."

I recognize the man now; he was at the reading ten years ago with the woman…his wife, Ophelia. The reading was done at this apartment before August and I lived here, because the big family house was being renovated.

I keep my voice level, "If you think we're going to tell you where they are just because you have a knife, guess again."

A kitchen knife floats through the air and hovers inches from the man's body.

The man laughs as if he expected August to try that. "Oh… No, you see…I'm not stupid. My whole body has a shield around it too, thanks to the witch. I know more about you Whitlocks than you think."

The kitchen knife clatters to the floor. August snarls and charges toward the man.

"NO!" I shout and rush toward my cousin.

The masked man slashes August's chest before August is able to forcefully twist the man's wrist, causing the knife to fall to the floor. I shove August out of the way and push the man up against the wall—hard. I punch him three times in the face until blood gushes from his nose and mouth.

"Don't you *ever* touch my cousin," I growl in his face. He slumps to the ground, unconscious. At least, I think he's unconscious. I crouch down and put two fingers on his neck and look for a pulse. There is one. I then whip around to check on August, and my heart skips a beat when I see blood seeping through his T-shirt.

"Fuck." I pull out my phone, dial 911, and quickly explain the situation to the operator. My cousin needs a hospital—and fast.

I sprint over to August and wrap my arm around his side. I walk with him leaned on my side outside to my car, but my tires are slashed. The intruder thought of all scenarios.

"Shit. Shit. Shit." I don't think an ambulance will get here fast enough. The hospital is five miles away. There's only one thing to do. Parked next to my car is August's sport bike. August keeps a cover over it with a lock, so the man probably didn't think he had to time to slash the tires. Sometimes when August gets home late, he sleeps with his keys still in his pocket. I hope this was one of those times. I sift through his sweatpants pocket and I almost sigh in relief as I pull out his set of keys. I unlock the cover, and quickly shove it off the bike. I grunt as I lift August onto the backseat, and I buckle him in. Luckily, when August purchased the bike, he had leather buckles installed. Not for him, but for our younger cousins. To keep them safe if they ever chose to ride it.

"Stay with me, August," I whisper. He groans in response as his head lolls to the side.

I climb onto the seat in front of him and start the bike.

"Am I... going to die?" August's voice is barely audible. His words grab onto my heart.

"No." I tell him confidently, trying to convince him... and myself.

The alternative is unfathomable.

I park the bike outside of the hospital and burst through the front doors and scream for a doctor. I'm holding August upright with all my strength. His skin is now pale and greenish. "It's gonna be okay," I murmur to him.

A nurse rushes over, quickly assesses his wound, and advises me to stay in the waiting room. She and another nurse wheel him to a room on a gurney. I take a seat in one of the waiting room chairs and rub my hands down my face.

He'll be okay.

I think about calling Opal, but I check the time, and it's five in the morning. After everything blows over, which will hopefully be sooner rather than later, I will tell my father and uncles, but not before then. And I'm definitely not cluing in Dawson or Felix.

The police have probably arrived at the apartment by now and taken the man away. I explained the situation to the operator as well as I could over the phone.

I'll drive myself crazy sitting here alone just thinking over everything. Maybe I will text Opal.

I slide a hand through my hair and turn my phone over in my palm.

Took August to the hospital... I'm fine, in waiting room. Miss you.

After I send the text, I drop my phone in the seat next to me and wait.

And wait.

And wait.

August has gotten himself into plenty of trouble over the years, but never anything involving a knife or a hospital visit.

My phone buzzes in the seat. I turn it over to see that Opal is calling me. A feeling of relief warms my chest. I answer.

"Eli?" Her voice is a mixture of grogginess and worry.

"I'm okay... I was just missing you."

I hear her starting to shift. "Tell me what happened, please. By the way, I'm coming."

I tell her what happened, and as soon as we hang up, one of the nurses walks toward me. I stand up from my seat and hope for the best.

"He'll be okay. He just needs to rest. We were able to stop the bleeding. He just needed a few stitches." She smiles warmly and directs me toward the room he's in.

21

OPAL

I walk backward, a cup of coffee in each hand, as I push open the hospital's entrance doors. I look like literal shit right now, but it's my girlfriend duty—or maybe my *soulmate* duty—to be here at the crack of dawn with Eli...for Eli.

I stop at the front desk and ask for directions to August's room. I follow the directions I'm given by the borderline-rude woman.

I don't like mornings either, lady.

I slowly walk into the room. Eli is sitting in a chair to the left of August with his hands clasped. August's eyes are closed. I tap Eli on the shoulder and hand him one of the coffees. He smiles gratefully. I quietly pull up another chair next to his and cup my coffee between my palms.

"How's he doing?" I whisper.

Eli takes a sip of his coffee. "The nurses say he'll be okay... just needed some stitches."

Good. I nod and gently squeeze Eli's forearm. "And how are you?"

"Better than him... Something's not right, Opal." Eli's gaze is pinned on August.

I shift in my seat. "What do you mean?"

Eli clutches the cup and meets my eyes. "You know when you have a bad feeling? Well, I guess it would be amplified for people like me... But yeah, something just isn't right, and I can't pinpoint what it is."

I nod slowly and refrain from questioning the actuality of gut feelings. "Whatever it may be, we'll get through it together." I give him a peck on the cheek. "Did they catch the guy?"

"Shit. I don't know. I need to call the dispatcher." He runs a hand through his hair as he rises from his seat. He takes a glance at August before turning toward the door.

"I'll come with you." I hold the door open for him as we make our way to the waiting room. Eli pulls his phone out of his pocket, and we both see a missed call.

"Maybe that's the police." Eli curses, dials the number, and holds the phone to his ear. I watch as he paces the room.

"He what?" Eli whispers hotly into the phone. He takes a deep breath and exchanges a few more words with the person on the other end of the line before he hangs up. He rakes a hand down his face and throws himself into a chair.

"What is it?" I rush over to sit next to him.

"He got away... He got *away*, Opal. I should've killed him."

I swallow the bile that threatens to rise. I clench my jaw. "Well, we'll find him." I cringe at the forced optimism in my voice.

"I didn't want to bring them into this, but I have to tell my uncles... Thank the Universe he doesn't know where they live... for now. Shit."

I struggle to find the right words to say and when I realize there are none, I pull Eli into a tight hug. Desperately hoping to hold him together.

"Um...August would like to see you." A nurse approaches us

and quickly looks between him and I. Eli pulls away from me and grabs my hand. We practically sprint to August.

We find August squinting at his outstretched hand.

"What is it, August?" Eli's question is clipped.

"I... can't." August is still squinting at his hand as he slowly rotates it in front of him.

"You can't what?" Eli presses, fear rising in his voice.

"My...telekinesis... It's gone." There's an edge to August's usually carefree tone.

"What do you mean it's *gone?*" Eli moves closer to August as if this will help him understand better.

"I mean it's gone." August stares wide-eyed at his palm and then at us.

"The knife," August whispers. "What the hell was in the knife?"

Realization dawns on Eli's face. Eli told me that the man said that he took the knife to a witch of some sort to block its physical powers. At this point, I'm not totally surprised that witches exist. I look to August and then to Eli. I see speculation and horror line their expressions. Now I not only believe in psychics but also in gut feelings, and something has gone terribly, terribly wrong.

What if the protection spell that was used on the knife can also be used to take away powers?

Is August's power gone because of it?

And the biggest mystery of all: where is the masked man now?

The room fills with a deadly silence as the fate of the Whitlock family screams unknown.

THANK YOU!

Thank YOU for picking up *Otherworldly*. It means the entire universe to me that you took a chance on Opal and the Whitlocks! Stay tuned for the next book in the series!

ACKNOWLEDGMENTS

Thank you to:

My fiancé, Dylan. I love you with all my heart; you're my real-life book boyfriend (fiancé).

My parents for supporting me unconditionally. Mom, thank you for always reading my work before I send it out into the world! Dad, thank you for showing me that there is more out there and introducing me to psychics and otherworldly shenanigans at a young age!

Talia. I'm glad we're able to live out our dreams together. I love you sister!

Hanna. Thank you for reading my stories and giving me encouraging and enthusiastic feedback. Follow her on Instagram (@authorhannacalloway), as she is due to publish a paranormal romance, *Royally Destined.*

My editor and friend, Kerri. You never fail to show me the way when I'm lost and encourage me when I need it the most. If you're looking for an editor or proofreader, check out her website: https://www.hqpeconsulting.com/!

Lastly, thank you, readers! You all push me to keep writing. I love you and thankyouthankyouthankyou.

ABOUT THE AUTHOR

Caroline Scott has always been a passionate soul ... passionate about stories, passionate about
  characters. She can't help but root for the underdog, a theme that weaves itself into her writing. When not writing, reading, or napping, Caroline loves to travel. A clear head and new experiences keep her creative juices flowing!

Follow Caroline on:

Instagram: @authorchs

Facebook: Author Caroline Scott

Printed in Great Britain
by Amazon